THIS WALKER BOOK BELONGS TO:

First published 1993 by Walker Books Ltd
87 Vauxhall Walk, London SE11 5HJ

This edition published 1995

2 4 6 8 10 9 7 5 3 1

This book has been typeset in Bembo Bold.

Printed in Hong Kong

British Library Cataloguing in Publication Data
A catalogue record for this title is available from
the British Library.
ISBN 0-7445-3662-6

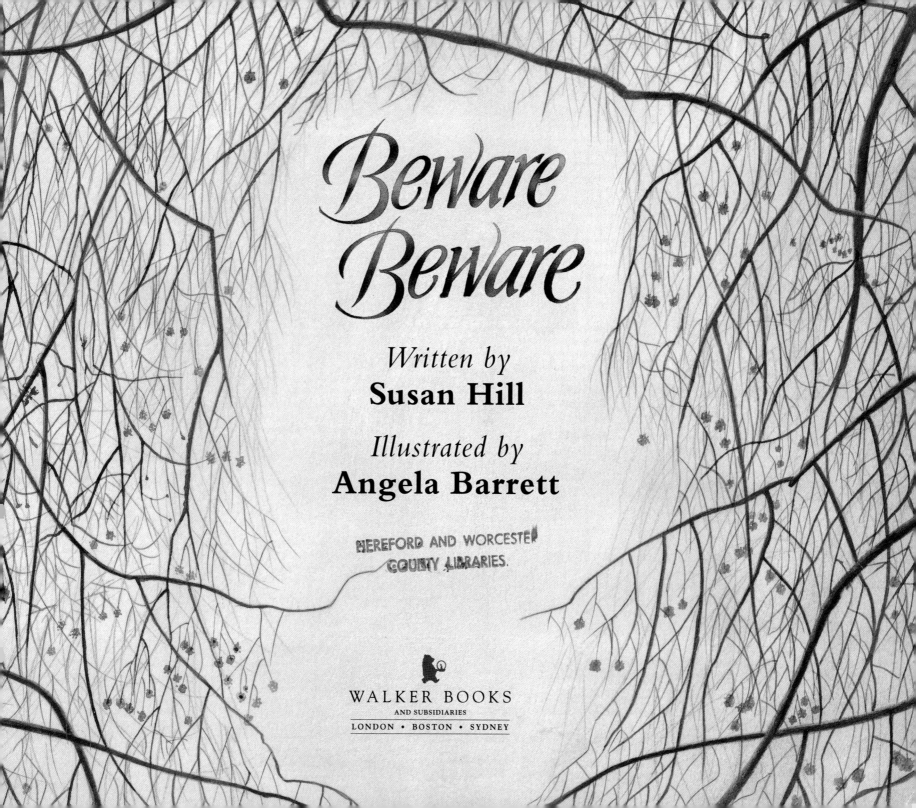

Beware Beware

Written by
Susan Hill

Illustrated by
Angela Barrett

WALKER BOOKS
AND SUBSIDIARIES
LONDON · BOSTON · SYDNEY

Kitchen's warm.

Smells of spice.

Kettle sings.

Fire bright.

But what's out there?

Beware, beware.

Setting sun

Rose red.

Light falls

Across the snow.

Path winds.

Who's to know?

Don't go!

But what's out there?

Slip down

Softly creep

Lift the latch

Snow's deep

In long shadow lies the wood.

I knew I could!

I'm here, out there.

Beware, beware!

I will take care.

Birds cold
Branches bare
What's over there?

Not far.
I can look back
I'm taking care
I'm there! I'm there!

Twig cracks

Dead leaves

No snow in the wood

Quiet. Safe. Dry.

Good.

What's there? What's there?

Beware! Beware!

Trolls Goblins

Elves Sprites

Mysterious lights

Fingers beckon

Eyes stare

Wolf

Bear

Dragon's lair

Beware! Beware!

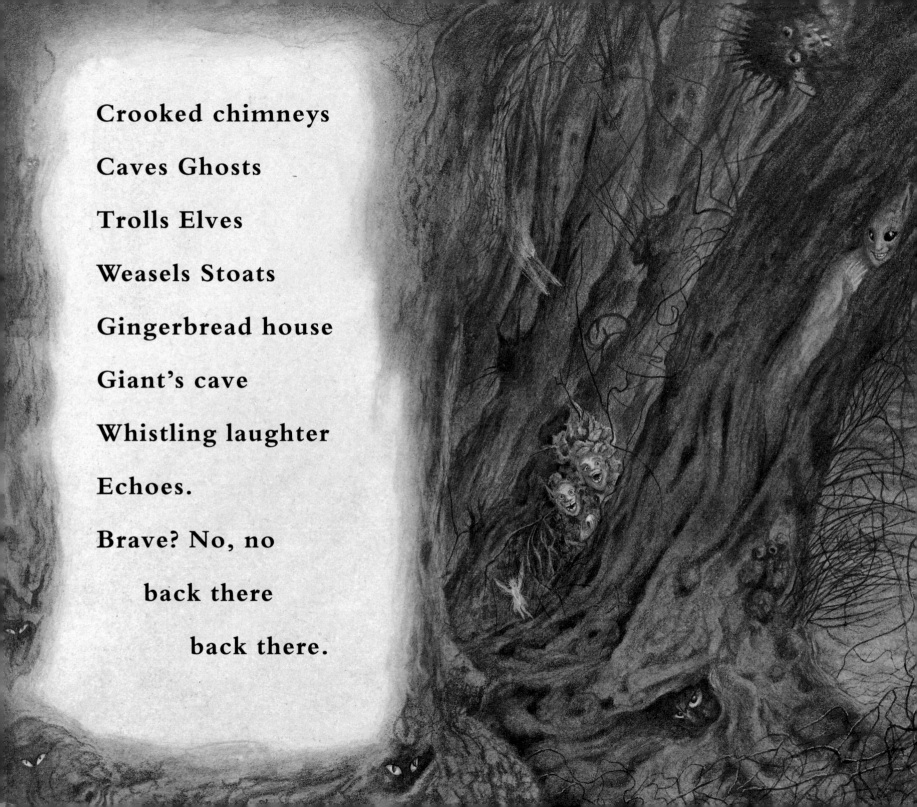

Crooked chimneys

Caves Ghosts

Trolls Elves

Weasels Stoats

Gingerbread house

Giant's cave

Whistling laughter

Echoes.

Brave? No, no

back there

back there.

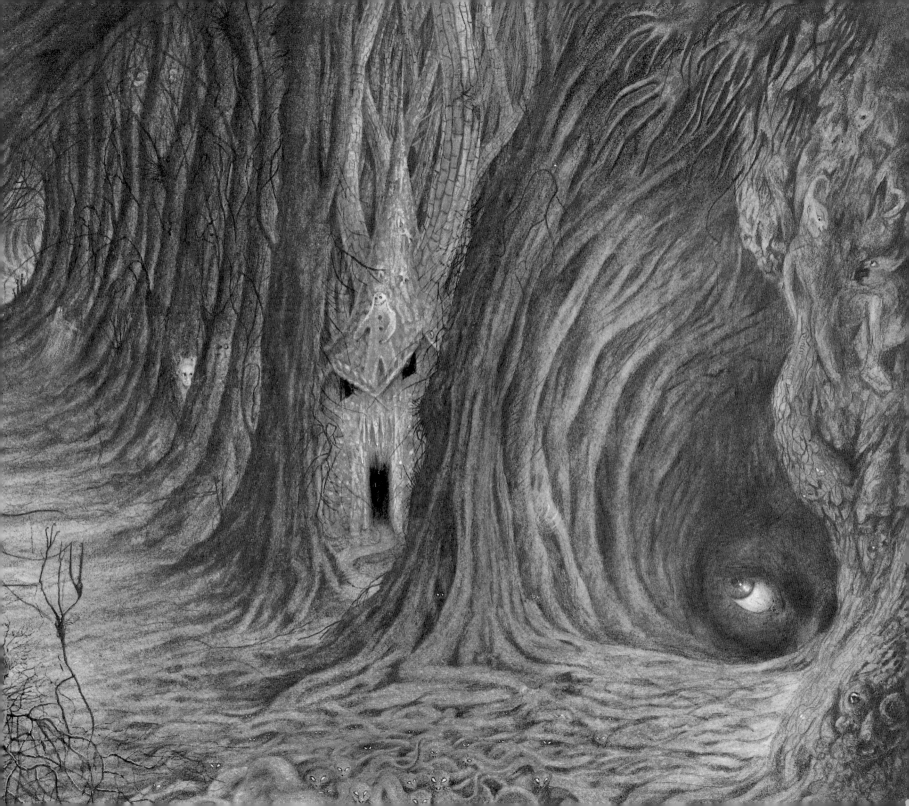

Oh, *where?*

Oh, there.

Kitchen's warm.

Smells of spice.

Curtains drawn.

Fire bright.

Night.

But *what's* out there?

MORE WALKER PAPERBACKS
For You to Enjoy

I WON'T GO THERE AGAIN
illustrated by Jim Bispham
"Susan Hill deals honestly and amusingly with a small boy's reactions
to his first days at nursery school... The text could not be bettered.
The book should help many very small children over early obstacles." *The Junior Bookshelf*
0-7445-2091-6   £3.99

SEPTIMUS HONEYDEW
illustrated by Carol Thompson
At three o'clock every morning, Septimus Honeydew wakes up and climbs into his parents' bed –
putting an end to their peaceful night's sleep. Things go from bad to worse –
until Aunt and Uncle Honeydew come to stay...
"The story, the characters and the drawings are charming."
School Librarian
0-7445-2346-X   £3.99

CAN IT BE TRUE?
illustrated by Angela Barrett
Winner of the Smarties Book Prize (6-8 years)
"Evokes, in a prose poem of marvellous concision, the real spirit of Christmas Eve ...
beautiful illustrations." The *Sunday Telegraph*
0-7445-1721-4   £3.99

Walker Paperbacks are available from most booksellers, or by post from B.B.C.S., P.O. Box 941, Hull, North Humberside HU1 3YQ
24 hour telephone credit card line 01482 224626

To order, send: Title, author, ISBN number and price for each book ordered, your full name and address,
cheque or postal order payable to BBCS for the total amount and allow the following for postage and packing:
UK and BFPO: £1.00 for the first book, and 50p for each additional book to a maximum of £3.50.
Overseas and Eire: £2.00 for the first book, £1.00 for the second and 50p for each additional book.
Prices and availability are subject to change without notice.